NIKKI MICHELLE

Scandalous (2)

Scandalous was previously released as Sexual Healing in the anthology Body Heat which is no longer available on Amazon.

Second edition

This book was professionally typeset on Reedsy.
Find out more at reedsy.com

Contents

Foreword

About this book...

In this book, you will meet characters who you will
see in future books by Nikki-Michelle. Several of
my original side characters also make small guest ap-
pearances in my partner in crime, Kai Leakes', books.
Many of our characters are best friends, associates,
and future lovers. We've chosen to connect a bit of
our literary world of our contemporary romances
together for you all to have a varied experience.

Preface

Now, before you get to thinking you're about to get an entrée, I must warn you, this is only an appetizer. My services aren't free, and my skill and reputation tend to speak for themselves. Don't be mad at me. Be mad at the game. I know the way I'm speaking may give some pause, as I'm a successful criminal defense attorney, but a part of my charm is that I can become a chameleon in any environment lucky enough to have my presence bestowed upon them.

Am I coming off too arrogant? Cocky even? Probably, but if I don't believe in me, who will? This will be only a glimpse into my life. I'll make it quick and easy for you. I'll also introduce you to my identical twin brother and a few of my favorite clients. I'll show you some of my most intimate moments and allow you to read my hidden secrets. Just when you desire to know what happens next, I'll pull out and leave you begging for more.

Welcome to the Gentelmen's Club...where no woman leaves unsatisfied...

One

Chapter 1

~~~

" I don't understand why you can't take me on as your client anymore."

I glanced at the woman standing naked in front of me. Her body was the stuff video girls were made of. She had thick thighs, a round plush backside, small curvaceous waist, and a perfect size D-cup chest that made the package all the more enticing. Her beautiful brown oval face, light brown doe-like eyes, and long waist-length locs also added to her beauty. She was the total package.

She was a beautiful Black woman; intelligent, strong willed, and she was independent. She knew all the right things to say to make any man feel like a king in bed. She'd also been a top client of mine for the last three years. However, I wasn't concerned with that. In my line of work, honesty was a requirement. It was not an option. When my clients started to lie to me, problems arose. And the one thing I did not need was problems.

I stood from the edge of the California king-sized bed then adjusted my purple label blue blazer. "You broke rule number one, Saniaa, and what's rule number one?" I asked her as I turned to the big wall mirror adjusting my platinum cuff links.

"Rule number one is not to ever lie to you about anything, especially not about having a significant other but—"

"No buts, Baby. I made that clear time and time again. This meeting is your last meeting."

I looked behind me as my phone beeped on the round wood grain table. Money had been transferred to my account. I'd gotten fifty-thousand two days before. The next hundred thousand that came through was like a severance package for me. The fact that she didn't realize I'd charged her extra or paid attention to that fact told me that although she'd read the rules, she hadn't paid attention to them. I was actually more pissed than I was letting on. I had a long list of clients who I catered to, and if even one fucked something up, it had potential to have a trickledown effect. I couldn't, and wouldn't, risk that. My other clients had paid top dollar just as she had, and they deserved my discretion just as she did. She broke a rule. Not only did she break the rule, but she broke my number one rule.

I was what regular people would call a male escort, but that was my second job. My first job was being a lawyer. By day I ran a law firm with my identical twin brother. In the exclusive Gentlemen's Club that I belonged to, it was essential that we set up rules so that none of the women who we provided services to got too comfortable. There were only a select few of us and each of us had our own set of clients that we accommodated.

There are a few ground rules, which are as follows: 1) Never lie to me. If a client lies to me, even once, for whatever reason, their contract is null and void. 2) Half of my fee must be paid two days before our scheduled meeting, the second half on the day of our scheduled meeting. 3) Make sure to keep your pussy clean, nice and neat at all times. A gynecological examination is required prior to the first meeting. That examination must include a full-scale testing of every STD, including HIV. No exceptions. 4) Never call my phone and try to hold a conversation with me. The only thing that needs to be said is the private code to let me know you're ready for our next meeting. 5) No other women are invited to our party. 6) I do not provide services to men. No exceptions. 7) A client must never get addicted to this dick or how it makes them feel. They must never mistake a good dick down for love. It is the quickest way to get their contract terminated. 8) Never refer anyone to me without my permission. 9) All clients must be able to afford me, no exceptions. I do not negotiate my price. 10) All gifts are very much appreciated; however, they do not compensate as payment. A client could buy me a house, a car, a seventy-foot yacht, which three of my clients had done already, but I still wanted my money. As stated before I do not negotiate prices. They were set. They were what they were and that was that. Refer to rule number 9. 11) All applications must be approved by the CEO of the Gentlemen's Club. They must also consent to a thorough background check. Failure to comply will garner them no response from me.

Rule number one was put into place mostly because just like women, men got jealous too. They would go through phones, emails, whatever to ensure their woman wasn't cheating on them. In addition to keeping an eye on significant others, I also needed to be sure my clients didn't have other surprises, like new boyfriends or crazy exes who would sneak up on me. I rubbed my big, tanned hands together as I watched myself in the mirror.

My looks had always worked in my favor. I had an appearance that most considered exotic. My mother was a beautiful Black-American woman with Caribbean and Choctaw Indian heritage, father was Aztecan or Mexica, but not Mexican. My butterscotch golden skin always got compliments. Long silky jet-black hair flowed down to the middle of my back. Grayish-blue eyes stared back at people when they looked at me.

Women had always told me I had eyes like that actor Michael Ealy. I'd never given it much thought. My eyes were what they were depending on the mood I was in. I stood at six feet five inches tall, my stomach played host to six perfectly toned pack of abs. Just below those abs sat a picture-perfect Adonis line that made any woman privileged enough to lay eyes on it swoon, especially when they would see what hung just underneath. I had long thick fingers that all of my clients begged me to use on them. Because of the business I was in I kept my body in shape, inside and out.

Saniaa ran to jump in front of me after I slid my feet into my designer loafers. "I've said I'm sorry over and over," she begged as she grabbed me at both creases of my arms. "I didn't know he would do that. I had no idea he was even back in town," she continued to plead her case. Her sandy blonde locs swung from side to side as she tried to get me to hear her out.

During the three years she'd been my client I'd learned that she and her husband were on the verge of divorce. He'd taken her self-esteem and toyed

5

with it. By the time she'd gotten around to calling me for my services all she'd wanted was for a man to confirm that she was desirable, that she was wanted.

She'd gotten my number from one of my other clients. It was rare that I allowed permission for a client to release my information to a potential one. Most times to even get me to have dinner with a client cost them a good twenty grand. My time was precious and being that I was damn good at what I did it would cost them to tell me why I should take them on as my client. But back to Saniaa and why she could no longer be my client.

Her husband was an asshole. There were times I just didn't understand us males. Saniaa was a beautiful woman and it was apparent she took pride in her appearance. She always kept herself in tip top shape. Judging by the things she'd confided in me and just by getting to know her I could tell that she got off on catering to her man. Most times when we met at our secret location all she'd wanted to do was show me how much she appreciated what I could give her. She always wanted to show me how much she appreciated me. She was a pleaser. So, for the life of me, I didn't understand why her husband didn't see what a true gem she was. Women paid me to pleasure them so whatever their pleasure, I provided. Saniaa's pleasure was pleasuring me in any shape, way, form, or fashion.

Don't get me wrong, I had to turn her out, too. So anytime she was in my presence I made sure to take time to kiss her, taste her, touch her, fuck her in any position she could handle…most of them she couldn't. I loved making a woman feel good. That giggle that a woman would give just because I winked at her was everything. Most men were completely clueless about all of the small things that could drive a woman mad. Saniaa's husband was one of those men. That was why she used his hard-earned money to pay me.

She never mentioned to me that along with her husband that she had another boyfriend on the side. No, that wasn't what pissed me off. What pissed me off was the fact that she'd allowed him to follow her to meet me for dinner one night. That boyfriend that she'd forgotten to mention walked up on my twin brother thinking it was me.

I guess he'd watched us long enough to know what I looked like. Now, while my brother and I were identical in looks that was where most of our similarities ended. My brother was not a fighter, not that he couldn't fight, he just refused to. So when he was confronted by Saniaa's boyfriend, not only was he was completely caught off guard, he didn't even have time to defend himself against a man who was obviously pussy whipped.

It was a problem that I had to address. And it had

to be addressed a.s.a.p.

"Don't beg, Saniaa. It's not attractive," I calmly told her then move away from her. "You knew the moment you lied to me that this was going to happen."

She quickly scrambled back in front of me. Her big, beautiful breasts bouncing along the way. "Please, I'll pay you more. I'll give you whatever you want just don't cut me off."

Were those tears I saw sparkling in her beautiful eyes? She'd often told me that I was her drug. That had also become a problem, but I'd let her get away with that broken rule. Yes, I had a rule about becoming addicted to the services I provided, mostly the dick. If I ever felt as if a client was becoming dependent on my sex, then I would cut her off with no question. The reason for that was because when a woman became addicted to a man, she could become a pain in the ass. Then she'd start to mistake a good dick down for love.

They would start to assume that I felt the same about them. That couldn't happen because I for damn sure didn't love not one of my clients. I loved pussy, sex, and money. They provided all three. I'd let Saniaa get away with that shit because out of all my clients, she was the one who was most consistent and most loyal. She was the one who I could count on like clockwork to hit my private line every third

Friday of the month with the code letting me know she needed her "fix" as she had called it.

It was never just about providing a woman good dick because truth be told they could have probably gotten that anywhere. No, what we provided in the Gentlemen's Club I belonged to was more than sex. We provided comfort. We provided an illusion, a fantasy for what women wished they could get in their everyday lives. Whatever our clients wanted for the time we were together, we provided. If she wanted to feel like she was the only woman in the world, we made it our business to ensure that she did. Fuck you, pay me. That was how it would always go.

I didn't do what I did for the money, though, not solely. My day job provided for me nicely on that end to be honest. I did what I did for the love of women. I loved women plain and simple. I could thank my old man for that. All we used to ever see him do was cater to my mother. The smile he would leave on her face just from smacking her ass taught me how simple it was to please a woman. Not to say they didn't have their fights, because they did. However, my father had always known the right things to say to get my mother smiling again.

"There is nothing else that you can give me, Baby. Your time is up. You fucked up and now I will become a distant memory for you or a figment of your imagination. However you want to spin that to work for you is fine by me," I told her as I looked down at her then picked up the Movado watch waiting for me on the table to put it back on my wrist.

"So you're just going to walk away from this good pussy?" she asked in almost an outrage.

Another reason she had to go. She'd start to get too comfortable with what she thought she could say to me. And obviously she'd also gotten confused. I didn't give a damn about how good her pussy was, and it was good, but I had plenty more where that had come from. It was a classic example of why men in my profession should never break our own rules for any of our clients.

It could come back to haunt us. I wasn't her man or her husband so losing her sex didn't faze me one bit, but obviously she thought it would. It was time to remind her otherwise. I turned on her quickly, picking her up by her small waist then dropping her on the bed. We were on the 28th floor of the W Downtown Atlanta. Not our normal meeting place, but since it was to be our last time engaging in such activities together, it was my place of choice. The daylight that was left kept a little natural light shining through the floor-to-ceiling windows.

Saniaa's luscious breasts bounced and swayed as she fell back on the big down covered bed. I gripped one of her ankles then snatched her to the end. I used my thighs to push her legs apart then pinned her wrists down above her head.

"Since you seem to have forgotten the rules, let me remind you of them. Your pussy means nothing to me anymore," I said to her.

She was no longer a client, so the fantasy was over. My brother had gotten attacked because she didn't keep up her end of the contract. I used my open palm to smack her pussy— hard—just the way she liked it. She moaned and arched, writhing around.

"Please, Saigon, just fuck me one last time," she pleaded, thrusting and grinding her hips like a mad woman.

She swung her head from side to side like she couldn't take what I'd done to her. Saniaa liked to be dominated. She got off on it. I slapped her pussy again, this time adding more pressure to her clit. She screamed out.

"Shut up. I didn't give you permission to scream. Did I?" I teased her through clenched teeth. "You've been a bad girl, Saniaa, and now you must be punished for it."

I looked down to see she was glistening with moisture already. I allowed her to feel the pleasure of my long, thick fingers playing with her one last time. After rubbing her yoni lips slow and aggressive, I two-finger strummed her clit then slid them inside

11

of her, allowing her juices to saturate my fingers and the bed. Once more, she screamed. And for disobeying a direct order, I smacked her lush thighs— right side, and then the left side. The hard slaps made her hiss. In a sense, I could say that I would miss this part of what she and I had shared. Her husband had outright refused to appease this side of her sexual nature. I had no problem with it.

"I said *shut up*. You do not have my permission to make a sound," I said in a low voice that came out more like growl. I leaned close to her lips. "You'll never be able to contact me again so don't try. All of the numbers you have will be changed."

Two of my fingers slowly slid back inside of her as my teeth toyed with her caramel-colored nipples. I bit down on each one, hard, giving her that rough kink she craved. I knew what she liked. I knew what would get her off. By the way her back arched and thighs clamped around my waist, I knew what was about to happen next. I lifted her a little more just to tilt her hips.

I was tapping against her g-spot, stroking in a motion against the place that gave her the most satisfaction. I knew when she was about to erupt because I felt her spot swelling. That deep firm massage against her spot, the massage that most of my clients begged for, was driving her crazy. The fact that she couldn't scream— wasn't allowed to make a sound— was also adding to her pleasure.

I quickly grabbed one of the thick bath sheets that we had left on the chair beside the bed. I knew what was about to happen but since I had no plans of taking my suit back off to fuck her again, I needed the towel to keep her juices from getting on my threads. After positioning the towel, I stopped stroking her spot then started to firmly tap at it. In no time her body released and sung my praises. No man had ever been able to read her body the way I'd come to. Before me she didn't know that feeling, that pressure mounting from when she was about to orgasm. It was me who encouraged her to relax then release. It was always a turn on to see a woman in tune with her body.

Still, not even with her stunning voluptuous body wriggling about on the bed would I indulge her any further. It was time for me to go.

"Fuck you then, Saigon," she yelled at me once she'd caught her breath. "You're just a whore anyway, a male whore who likes to pretend he isn't what he really is."

She was angry so I would let her say whatever it was she wanted to make herself feel better. Her southern accent had come out and she sounded every bit of the country bumpkin she really was. No matter the amount of time she'd taken after getting married to learn to articulate her words, when she was angry, the country girl in her came out. After I washed my hands, I grabbed my cell, attached it to the clip on my hip, and then walked to the door.

"I'll be that, Baby, but at the end of the day, I'm no longer available to be *your* whore. Goodbye, Saniaa."

As I made my way down the cappuccino-colored carpeted hall, I thought back to how I got started in the business. When I'd met the CEO of the company, he was twenty-seven and had walked into my office because he'd heard that my brother and I were the best criminal defense attorneys in Atlanta. He'd been looking for attorneys who he could trust, who he could use for his company. One to keep on retainer per se. That had piqued my interest. Why would a young Black male such as he need a criminal defense lawyer on retainer, especially when on paper he looked to have a legit company?

To my surprise he'd told me that he had his own file on me and my brother. He'd done his homework, too. He knew our ins and outs, how many cases we'd won, how many we'd lost. He even knew that I had a different woman for almost every day of the week, hence the reason he chose me and not my brother to talk to.

"Your brother seems cool enough," he said. "But it's you who I think would understand my plight better."

I studied the man before me just as intently as he studied me. "Have a seat and let me hear you out. Then

I'll let you know if I'm interested in representing you and your company."

I knew he was about business because of the way he dressed and the way he represented himself. But it was when I read through the file that he laid on my desk that my eyebrows shot up.

"Are you serious?" I'd asked. "This is what you do?"

He nodded. "It's what I do and because of that that I would like to have an attorney of your caliber on retainer."

For a moment, I sat and read over what was in the folder he'd given me. Every question I'd asked him he answered honestly. It was another reason I contemplated taking him on as a client. After he and I had spoken in depth and he'd assured me that no paper trail could come back to bite him in the ass, I decided to take him on.

It wasn't until a few months later when he approached me with the idea of joining the Gentlemen's Club. At first, I was a bit skeptical. I asked him what the hell did he think he was, a pimp? After he laughed and explained to me that he wasn't on that level of bullshit, I decided to give what he did a try. I must say that the business had been good to me.

Two

Chapter 2

༄

My love for women was my strength but as any wise man knew, it could also be a weakness. I stepped on the elevator that only had one other occupant. He was a male, about twenty-nine in age, according to my research, and five-eleven in height. The look on his face when he saw me was a puzzled one, like he couldn't believe I was up and walking around. To anyone else, his reaction would have been a strange one, but to me, it was expected. He was so shaken that he'd forgotten this was the floor he was supposed to get off on, letting the doors close with him still on the elevator.

The guy was the color of a brown paper sack grocery bag, but his nervousness gave a red tint to his cheeks that showed his guilt. As I'd pleasured Saniaa,

I snatched her cell phone from the table next to the bed and sent a text to the man I'd just stepped on the elevator with. He was the man who had attacked my brother. I could tell by the way he kept glancing at me over his shoulder that he was about to shit bricks. To me, there was nothing worse than a coward, those who committed certain crimes, but were afraid of the same things happening to them.

Sometimes it was bad having a twin when one wasn't sure what their other half had done to some-one. My brother had found that out most of our lives. And it was normally me who was getting him into trouble.

"Calloway, is it?" I asked him after he'd finally figured out that the elevator had stopped.

He turned to face me slow and easy. Although I could see that he was a coward, he tried to put on a tough act.

"I guess the first ass whooping you got wasn't enough for you?" he taunted after squaring his shoulders and lifting his chin.

There was a scar underneath his left eye. The clothes he wore looked as if they came from some runway in Paris. He was taking that whole urban metrosexual thing to another level with the tight leather pants that looked more like the leggings. The loose-fitting, purple sheer-like top along with the Chanel boots made him look queer. I couldn't see how the man before me was interested in women, but he was.

"One thing a man should never do is let a woman cloud his judgment," I said.

He fixed his mouth to say something. He could have actually said something, but I didn't hear him. My fist connected to his face. I wasn't a man who did too much talking in fighting situations. I was more about actions. My brother may not have been a fighter, but I had no problem with putting a man on his ass.

Calloway fell back against the elevator doors and I followed my punch with a swift kick to his right knee taking him down to the floor. He yelped then groaned out as he went down. His face was twisted in agony and pain. I wasn't attacking him because he'd come after me. No, I was doing it because I was feeling like shit that my brother had gotten dragged into the equation.

The next reason was because any man foolish enough to fight over a woman who was clearly fucking another deserved his ass handed to him. My knee connected to Calloway's face making blood spew like a slow running stream. I had to handle him and do it quick. The one thing I couldn't afford was the police to be pulled into the equation. All the men associated with what I did had too much to lose for one loose thread to cause it all to fall apart.

Calloway was down. I'd already called and asked the beautiful woman at the front desk to keep everyone off the elevator. It was easy to convince her because I was just that good. She was a natural beauty whose name tag read Kristen. All I did was convince her that it would be worth her time if she did me a little favor.

I pulled Calloway's limp body away from the doors then pressed the red emergency button to open them. Three white males and a black male stood there waiting on me.

"'Sup, Sai," the black one greeted.

I heard Calloway groaning in pain on the floor. I nodded, stepped over his body, and then exited the elevator. The four young males took my place. Just like I knew people in high places, I also knew people in low places.

"Handle that," I said before walking away.

"No, problem," one of the white males answered.

They were all from the street, had been my clients since they were sixteen. While I'd gotten them on the straight and narrow as best I could, I could take the boys out the hood, but I couldn't take the hood out the boys. I rounded the corner then smiled at Kristen as her eyes sparkled behind her glasses. She wanted to ask what I had done but was smart enough not to. The lobby wasn't too crowded. A few people milled about, some checking in, others checking out.

The heels of my loafer clacked the marble floor until I stepped onto the Oriental rug. I walked over to the front desk then slid Kristen my card across the counter.

"Call me," I told her as I proceeded to walk from the building.

There was no need to stay around longer than I was supposed to. She would be rewarded greatly for her service. Once outside, the warm air embraced me as a lover would. I hated it. The heat in Atlanta sometimes reminded me of the summers in Augusta on my grandparents' farm. I used to always feel as if I would catch heat stroke, especially when we would be out in the gardens.

I was happy to get into my car and crank up my air. I drove home in complete silence. There were no accidents on the road, so there was hardly any traffic. I made it home to Stockbridge in no time. My home was nestled in a cul-de-sac inside of a private elusive neighborhood called Lake Spivey Estates. All twenty-five thousand square-feet had been bought and paid for by the women I serviced monthly. It was one of many.

After I parked my car in the three-car garage, I hopped out and made my way inside. Cool air greeted me, and I was thankful. The alarm chimed then welcomed me after I put in my code. I was never one to waste my time bragging about how expensive the inside or outside of my home was. There was no need to do that. I lived comfortably and my home was lavished with the finer things.

I kicked my loafers off at the door. My dress socks did nothing to keep the cold of the Italian marble flooring from my feet. My home smelled of fresh linen and the left-over scent of orange chicken that I'd eaten the day before.

I had to admit, it was good to have taken care of my problem, because that meant I could focus on my other clients without having to worry about the one who had lied to me. I shouldn't have been surprised when my phone started to ring and it was The Judge. That was what I called that particular client because she was one of the most revered judges in Georgia. At just forty-five she'd managed to garner the attention that most judges had to work until they were damn near one foot in the grave to get. There was even talk about her possibly being nominated for the Supreme Court by the President. But of course, that could all fall apart if they knew that she paid me monthly to service her physical needs, the ones that her husband couldn't even come close to.

"You're ringing my private line, why?" I greeted her.

"I cannot believe you dropped my girl like that, Saigon. What gives?" She had a beautiful Girl 6 voice, one that made my manhood stir around in remembrance of our times together.

I chuckled as I made quick work of removing my shirt then taking refuge on my bed. A brother was tired. While Saniaa was no longer my client, she had worn my ass out. I had to always make sure I went to the gym to amp up and take a healthy green shake before going to her. She had been insatiable.

I propped one arm behind my head. "You know the rules, Judge. She had to go because she broke them."

She gave a light snicker. "How is Chad anyway? I don't know why he didn't fight back. What's the use of being trained as he is in martial arts and not use it?"

"You know Chad, he won't fight. He's always been like that. I think his dick gets hard knowing he can fuck his opponent up but doesn't. Maybe that's his ego trip. But he's doing well. Didn't really faze him."

She grunted then made a sound as if she moaned softly. "You know, I'd damn near sell my soul to get Chad in this business with you. Why won't he do it, San?"

She'd called me San, reminding me that she knew me personally, more so than any other client. I mentally rolled my eyes and ran a hand through my hair. She wouldn't have been the first woman to have a thing for my brother. If I hadn't been in

22

the same room when we lost our virginity, I'd think he'd never had any pussy. Chad wasn't like me. He was an introvert and didn't think it was that big of a deal to have a woman. He didn't worship the ground they walked on as I did, well, at least, not in the same way I did.

I mean he'd had girlfriends— and I did mean friends— here and there, but nothing serious as I saw it. Still, women threw themselves at him and were let down each time he respectfully declined. I had one girl in college tell me she was only dating me because she couldn't get him and that I was the next best thing. Would have crushed a lesser man's ego, but I fucked her anyway.

"Because he doesn't believe in what I do. He even hates the fact that I do it. Now, once again, why are you on my private line holding a conversation with me?" I asked.

She sucked her teeth and sigh hard. "Oh my goodness. You're such a dick. You'd think with all the money and clients I send your way you'd show a little more enthusiasm to hear from me."

"Judge, you have thirty seconds before I introduce you to the dial tone."

"Okay, damn. I have a new prospect for you."

"Oh, no, no. Hell no. You struck out with Saniaa. Your references are done."

"Oh, come on, San. I even cursed Saniaa out for

23

you, more so for Chad, but please, trust me on this one. She's legit."

I grunted my hesitation.

"So, listen," the Judge continued. "Dionne is thirty-nine with two kids and a husband. Her husband's sex isn't worth a damn. She doesn't want to leave him, but my girl is in serious need of a fix. She can afford you, so can I pass along your business card?"

I sat silently as I thought about it. It could never hurt to have another Bella Donna on my team.

"Okay, but if she fucks up, you're done," I said.

"Ha! You can never be done with me, San, and you know it. I'll pass along your info and you can go from there. MUAH! Talk soon, Babe," she said then giggled.

It was one of the things I liked about the Judge. She was a hard ass on the bench. She took no mess from anyone who stepped foot in her courtroom, but with me, she giggled, laughed, and acted like she didn't have to sentence hardened criminals daily.

For the rest of the day, I relaxed. There was nothing required of me at my law office with my brother. I had a few cases that needed my attention, but I needed to regroup and get my mind back on track.

After cooking a quick meal of steamed broccoli, salmon, and black rice, I sat in my front room and watched the ten o'clock news. It was something I did just to stay atop of things. As the night progressed, I worked out, dialed my parents to see how they were doing, and then I pulled out my case files. I decided to do a bit of work because I couldn't sleep. That was usually my routine anyway.

* * *

A week later, I found myself sitting in Chops Lobster Bar in Buckhead. The steakhouse was an Atlanta icon known for its steaks and exquisite seafood selections. I sat in the back in a black leather-adorned booth against the far-right wall waiting for my guest to arrive. I looked at my watch because, just as with everything else, I was punctual. When I set a time, I liked to keep it. My guest was already fifteen minutes late.

I sighed with annoyance and waived my waitress off as she was about to walk back over to refill my glass of water. Just as I was about to call it a night, I looked up to see my guest in question walking in. Now, she wasn't what I expected. Because the Judge knew what I liked, I was shocked at the woman wearing all white approaching me. It was required that all potential clients wore that color upon our initial meeting. Not only would it make them stand out among others in our meeting place, but to me, there was nothing sexier than a woman wearing white.

The woman, whose name was Dionne, walked with an air of confidence about her. She strutted in her all white— designer and tailored by the way it fit her— two-piece suit that contoured to her frame perfectly. She had the pearl earrings and necklace on that I'd sent to her job. Her hair was pulled back to the nape of her neck in a perfect bun. No make-up, her beauty was flawless; skin had been perfectly kissed by the sun. Lip gloss sparkled on her full lips.

Her head was held high, and I, like every other patron, stared on as if she was a superstar. A few brothers tried to get her attention. All of them were ignored. Two things about her immediately stood out; she was confident, and she was full figured. It was well known that most men down south loved their women with meat on their bones. I preferred my women a little smaller, no more than a size ten. My guest looked to be every bit of a curvy sixteen.

I stood, like the gentleman I was raised to be, as she approached. Once she made it to my table, she removed her designer sunglasses, and I was able to see her coffee brown eyes. Now, all eyes were on both of us. I knew I looked debonair in my tailor-made gray suit. My black Italian leather shoes looked like they were fresh from the cobbler.

Hair fell around my shoulders and down my back as it always did. Shirt was crisp and baby blue.

Cuff links reflected off the lights. I didn't believe in wearing neck ties so the top of my dress shirt was slightly opened. I smiled and reached out to lay one hand on her lower back as I leaned in to kiss her cheek. Now, most women would be shocked at my gentlemanly gesture. My guest acted as if she expected nothing less.

"Good evening, Dionne. Glad I could be your guest this evening," I said.

She returned the kiss then pulled back with a slight smirk on her features. "Thank you. I'm glad you could as well."

I chuckled at her arrogance. She was well-spoken, slight southern accent with a little mid-west in there, and she smelled of vanilla spice. I waited until she was seated before I sat back down. I paid close attention to her as she ordered from the menu. Rockefeller oysters for starters and a bottle of their finest wine told me that she had been there before. Once she was done, she turned to look at me with that same light smirk on her face.

"So, Saigon, let's get right down to business, shall we? No need for the pretenses," she said.

I raised a brow. I was normally the one to get things started, but I played along, just to see where things would lead. She was assertive. Something I wasn't used to with the women I dealt with. Most of my clients came to me needing their egos stroked and self-esteemed lifted. Yes, even the Judge had needed that.

"Okay, let's get down to business," I said.

"Basically, you know why I'm here. First thing first, I love my husband. Would never leave him. That's why I sought out your services."

None of what she had said mattered to me since I didn't care if she wanted to leave her husband or not. I told her as much.

"You're here because in order for me not to leave him, I'm going to need some satisfying sex. He doesn't do that for me. I would rather cheat than to leave him. And I know that doesn't make sense to you," she said as she picked up one of the cloth black napkins and wiped the evaporating water from her glass before taking a sip. "But it makes perfect sense to me and that's all that matters."

"Okay."

"Now, I've read all of your rules and requirements. I have no fault with any of them," she said as she reached inside of her Chanel bag.

I watched in amusement as she slid a manila folder across the table to me. "What's this?" I asked, not touching the folder, but leaning back to watch the woman before me.

"That is a printout of my visit to my gynecologist today, along with my history from the last year. With that you will find a cashier's check for your retainer fee. That's what we'll call it, Mr. Santiago."

My head slowly tilted to the side at the name she called me. She looked down at her watch like she was pressed for time. I remained silent. I didn't know what to make of the woman. I didn't know whether to be appalled or impressed. I could tell she was used to being in control. She was the type of woman who no man could tell what to do. She was accustomed to having things go her way, which probably intimidated her husband in the bedroom.

When men felt intimidated by their women, it showed in areas not readily thought of. In my mind, I was picturing her riding her husband for dear life, trying to make it to her finish line before he made it to his. I didn't even know if I would take her on as a client, so the fact that she'd already brought a "retainer" amused me inwardly. That meant she was certain of herself.

I'd taken the time over the course of the week to get to know the woman who had potential to be a client. She was a top-level executive at Charter Marketing firm before they'd merged with a bigger firm. Now, she spent her time working for a top record label as their head marketing director. That was a formidable job for a woman her age, but she was used to it obviously having had worked at Charter. She and her husband had been married fresh out of high school. They'd had twins their freshmen year of college. I had to admit, I was surprised to see that kind of love. Stories like that usually ended with a single mother and a bitter man. She loved to read, got a kick out of being a soccer mom, and refused to speak to her own mother. Dionne was a made woman, one who had made herself.

"By the way, I know Saigon is your middle name and not your surname. I know you have set up these little rules that I find quite comical being that you're paid dick," she quipped so fast that I had to frown and lean forward just to make sure I heard her correctly.

"Excuse me?"

She chuckled deeply then leaned forward. "Yes, you heard me. You're paid dick, so you having all these little rules as if you're not the side piece tickles me. And please tell me you're not offended, Santiago, and yes I'll call you that because I refuse to call you by the name all your other "clients" call you."

"Ms. Mills, I can tell you right now that whatever you're assuming you know about what it is that I do, you don't. I'm no one's paid dick. I do what I do for the love it and because I want to. Nothing more. Nothing less. All clients that come to my firm never leave unsatisfied," I corrected her.

"So, why don't you do it for free?" she asked with her right brow raised.

I didn't respond right away, as the waitress had

come back with wine. Once she was done garnishing our glass with the sweet red wine, I turned my attention back to Dionne.

"You love your job, don't you?" I asked her.

"That I do."

"So why don't you do it for free?"

"My job is quite different from yours, Santiago. I'm not a paid piece of side ass."

"I'm a lawyer."

"You're a side-ho, a male whore."

I chuckled then thumbed my nose. I knew her kind. She was trying to rile me. And no matter how annoyed I was, there was no way I would admit openly or otherwise to what my services really were.

"If that were true, that would make you a trick, a female John."

A crude smile eased across her lips. "Good, now that you know your position and mine, I have a few rules of my own."

At first, I chuckled, then I laughed so loudly as I leaned back in my seat that other patrons turned to glance at us. She joined me in laughter as she reached back, undid her bun and shook her head from side to side. Her natural brownish mane came undone. She then took the pearls from her ears and neck and slid them across the table to me.

"First thing, I don't accept gifts from you. You're not my man. You're a hired dick that I call from time

31

to time to satisfy my urges, nothing more, nothing less. I have my own money, can buy my own gifts. Don't need yours. If anyone is to be giving gifts, it will be me. Please don't call me, I'll call you. Keep that in mind for the future, okay?" she asked then took a sip of her wine. "Next, I'll make the dates where I want you to be available, not the other way around. I'm paying you for a service, so you don't get to choose when I can get them. If I call, I need you to be available, especially if my money is taking care of you. Got that?"

Now, under any other circumstances my dick may have been hard, and I'd be pressed to get Dionne to a room to make her break every rule she had just set into place, but something about the way she was trying to handle me turned me off.

"I see you have the game all wrong. I'm not hired dick. I'm a lawyer and my services and reputation speak for themselves. If hired dick is what you want, then I suggest you Google a male escort service or something," I calmly told her.

For some reason the way she was coming at me put my senses on alert. She was too free in calling me paid dick.

She smoothly finished off her wine, took the black cloth napkin and wiped the corners of her mouth. What she did next, I didn't expect. She stood and slowly unbuttoned her suit jacket then her blouse. Her breasts were glorious and bountiful as they spilled out the cups of her bra. Her measurements set everything male in me on alert. Dionne's rounded hips set out like beacons of pleasure.

I picked up my glass of wine, yet amused, and took a sip. The sweet tangy taste of the wine coated my palate. "What are you doing?" I asked, sure the other patrons were thinking the same.

Most of the men couldn't keep their eyes off her perfect breasts as they sat buoyantly in a black lace bra. All I could think was that I was glad no children were around and how I wanted to see what those breasts looked like once the bra came off.

"I wanted you to know I'm not wearing a wire. I'm not the feds, or the cops, or the CIA, or whichever branch of the law you're worried about. If you would like you can run your fingers through my hair to assure no wire is there either. I would strip naked, but I'm sure you wouldn't be able to handle it."

By the time she'd sat back down the waitress was dropping off the plate of oysters that she'd ordered. I declined when the waitress asked me if I wanted to order anything. I asked her for another glass of water then turned my attention back to Dionne. I was surprised to see that she was preparing to leave.

"You didn't eat your food," I said to her.

After she finished buttoning her blouse, she put her glasses on and smiled at me. "Those are for you.

You'll need them anytime I call you. I suggest you try them with Tabasco sauce for an extra kick if you get my meaning."

She stood and grabbed her purse. I slid the folder back over to her and watched as she opened it and removed all her paperwork from the doctor. No way would I touch the cashier's check inside. One reason was because I still didn't trust her. Another was because I wouldn't be taking her on as a client. She spelled trouble and I didn't have time for trouble. She threw down five-hundred-dollars on the table and walked out of Chops like she hadn't just almost flashed half of the establishment.

Three

Chapter 3

∽ೞಲೞ∽

"Oh my God, Saigon, why do you do this to me?"

I was ten and a half inches deep inside of K. Michelle. No, not the love-disheartened singer, her look-a-like. The one thing that stood out most about her was the way she could croon out my name inside of a moan. She loved for me to be on top, between her thick luscious thighs, stroking in and out of her body like she was mine. One of her French manicured hands pulled at her own hair. Her mouth was half mast, eyes wide, back arched, and hips rocked back and forth in fervor as she climaxed. She'd always told me nobody could make her have an orgasm like I could. Not even the man she laid with every night. As a friend of mine once said, 'there was nothing like making another man's woman moan out your name'.

Simone had been my client for the last ten months. She wasn't married like my other clients. She'd been in a long-term relationship with one of the Atlanta Falcon's most talked about running backs. All she wanted was to get married, have children, and become a football/ stay-at-home wife. She wasn't your typical sport's wife or non-wife that people saw on VH1 and the like. She was hardworking, determined, and driven. She did more than fuck a baller, have a baby by him, and tried to become a millionaire. She'd actually refused to push out a baby by him until he married her. But just like all my other clients, something was lacking. She needed romance. Needed to feel like she wasn't throwing her life away on a dead-end relationship.

That was where I came in. After I'd taken her on a private jet to lunch in New York, we flew back to Atlanta where I romanced her further. I had my driver take us around town, walked around the park, bought her some roses from a street vendor, ran through the geysers at Centennial Park, and caught a matinee at the Old Fox Theatre in downtown Buckhead. The theater only showed old black and white movies, which she loved.

Back in high school, she dreamed of becoming a movie director. She loved all the old Agatha Christie and Hitchcock type films. So, after the movies, I took her down to a friend of mine's movie studio and let her direct herself a mini-movie. The smile on her face and glee in her eyes let me know that I'd given her the fantasy she longed for. That was what I did. I provided fantasies. And when it was all over, my clients, my Bella Donnas, my lovers, had to leave me and go back to their reality.

It had been over two weeks since I'd met Dionne. No word. No call from her. Nothing. I'd at least expected her to ask the Judge as to why I hadn't given an answer to her question of becoming my client. She presented a challenge, one I found myself wanting to take on. I'd called the Judge that day and told her to let Dionne know I would be taking her on as my client. If for no other reason than I wanted to make her eat her words.

Friday rolled around and I found myself at the gym. I'd seen all of my professional clients for the week and my weekend would be dedicated to one of my clients. I was working out, sweating like a slave because, just like my clients, I needed that release. I was getting pumped up in preparation of seeing her. Delana was a classy chick who believed that she was entitled to the finer things in life. That included me. I chuckled every time I thought about how she became my client. It was the only time it could be said that I snatched a woman from my brother's grasp so unabashedly. I was greedy and selfish most times. My brother knew this so, he wasn't fazed in the least.

I was in the middle of thinking about how I talked Delana into paying for my services and walking into the locker room when my cell rang. I knew it was Delana telling me she was at our meeting place. That woman was crazy, but in a good way. I loved that she was honest as hell, always wanted me to know that if she could have both me and my brother she would. Something that always slightly annoyed me but made me respect her more for the honesty. Besides, I was used to it. It didn't bother...most times. But what did bother me was when I picked up my phone and there was a text from Dionne.

Are you available today? the text read.

My right brow rose, and my head tilted. Did she not read the contract?

You didn't make an appointment. I responded.

When she didn't text back right away, I headed to the shower. Washed my hair and my ass. Oiled my body up and down and donned a pair of designer dress slacks with the same designer polo style shirt. I slid my dress socks-clad feet into some LV loafers and then headed out the gym. It was a sunny day in the A. As usual women of all racial backgrounds and ethnicities openly admired me. I chuckled as one joked about pulling on my hair as I fucked her. Yeah, women in the A were bold like that.

Just as I made it to my truck, my cell vibrated again.

I don't need an appointment. Money has been delivered. I expect to see you at this hotel in thirty minutes.

Is this woman out of her mind? I thought. She was trying to handle me. I guess it was because she was telling herself as long as she treated our arrangement like it was only a business transaction then she could go through with it. After all, she did come to our initial meeting declaring her love for her husband. Still, I couldn't shake the curiosity that was getting the best of me. There was something in me, maybe male pride, that wanted to see just what made her think she could handle me like she was trying to do. She was obviously used to running shit and having her way. When my phone alerted me that the funds had indeed been transferred to my bank account, I locked the address into my GPS and decided to head to where she was.

It didn't take me long to get to Drury Inn & Suites. I knew us meeting at that quaint little hotel wasn't going to work. It wasn't my style and I never took any of my women to such places. I always wanted my clients to feel like they were special, and this shit looked like peasant quarters. The brown and tan brick building looked to have no more than seven floors. The parking lot was scarce. To my left traffic was light up and down Jonesboro Road. The hotel sat off behind a set of railroad tracks. I knew this side of town, just didn't hang out there much. I grabbed my keys and my phone then exited my truck. I made my way into the lobby and shook my head. While it was clean and welcoming, it reminded me of a country cottage with the way it was decorated.

"Welcome to Drury Inn & Suites. Will you be staying with us today?"

I gave a head nod and smiled at the dainty greasy haired white girl behind the marbled welcome desk. I wasn't one to make an announcement about my arrival to any place. I spoke, said I was meeting someone and kept it moving. My mind fucked with me the whole time I made my way to the elevators. If curiosity killed the cat, then what the fuck was it about to do to the dog? Still, that didn't deter me. I stepped off onto the seventh floor and made my way to the room number she'd sent me.

I knocked once and she opened the door like she had been standing there waiting for me. The room was drab. The king-sized bed was made up with a spread that looked like something Kanye's baby mama wore to the Met Gala. The floor had dingy, but clean red carpeting with gold specks. Two red cushioned chairs sat off in each corner. In between was a small round wooden table. The small flat screen TV sat on top of a wood grain dresser and that was all there was to the room.

At that moment, however, nothing mattered because before me stood Dionne and she was as naked as the day she had come into the world. Her thighs touched when she walked but they were toned. She had a small fupa and slick, minimal hair to cover her pussy. And her breasts? Her breasts were everything I thought they would be out of her bra. They were plump, juicy, and perky. She had dark brown areolas and her nipples were as big as chocolate morsels. Her natural hair cascaded around her shoulders. I licked my lips because there was no way I could lie and say I didn't like her presentation.

As I coolly slid my hands in my pockets, I said, "I could have gotten you a better room than this."

"I don't need a better room," she said. "All I need is a bed with clean sheets and you to do what I'm paying you to do."

"So you want me to treat you like a whore?"

"No, I'm treating you like a whore. I want you to work for your money."

Dionne was tall for a woman, at least five-nine. She stood with her hands on her ample round and shapely hips. Toes were French manicured, and she smelled like she had bathed in cocoa butter. My pride had me wanting to turn around and walk the fuck out, but the male in me had me reaching out to pull Dionne close to me.

"Don't kiss me. You're not my man. I don't need

41

foreplay. My pussy's already wet because I'm horny and I haven't had a good dick down in years," she said.

I watched with heady vision as she sat down on the bed and then laid back. She placed her feet flat on the bed before spreading her legs. I'd come across a lot of pussies in my day, but none made me want to fall and worship it. Her pussy was squeaky clean. Her pearl was peeking through. It was plump and my mouth watered wanting to suck on it and see what her juices would taste like.

She took her fingers, stuck two in her mouth then brought them down to stroke her own kitty. "Stop playing around and give me what I paid for."

Her assertiveness, in the moment, turned me on. There was nothing like a woman who knew what she wanted and wasn't afraid to go after it. It didn't take me long to get out of my clothes. I didn't make a show of it. Just stripped down to my bare minimums. Her wide-eyed reaction once all my clothes came off let me know I was back in the driver's seat. I chuckled low which annoyed her because she told me to shut the hell up. As she laid on the bed, still sucking her juices from her fingers, I grabbed the magnum box she had laying on the bed and donned a condom over my rigid dick.

She didn't want talking. She didn't want foreplay. She didn't want affection. She was different than the

42

women I normally dealt with, but in the same breath, she wasn't. All of my clients came with a fantasy of what they wanted me to be to them. Dionne's fantasy was for me to be her side-dick. That was it. Nothing else. No fancy shit. No words of adoration or words telling her how beautiful she was. She didn't need that. Her husband could give her all of that. He just couldn't deliver the dick down that she wanted. And just like I provided fantasies for the other clients in my little black book, I'd give her what she wanted too.

That was my reasoning as I crawled on the bed and caged her between my arms. I looked down into the face of the woman who demanded I fuck her like I hated her and nothing more. She talked mad shit, but that gasp she gave out just as my head broke skin told me that underneath all that big talk, she was a woman in desperate need of satisfaction. I smirked. She was a woman who loved a man who couldn't get her to the place that she was longing for.

I played with her like that for a while. Just short stroking her. Put my dick not even halfway in, slow stroking then pulling out just to watch her reaction over and over. My sex was good and I knew that. Sex game was on point because of all the practice I'd had. And in that moment, she felt it too. Her hands gripped my long hair and yanked hard forcing me to grit my teeth.

43

"Gotdamn...the Judge was right. Shit, nigga, your dick..." was all she was able to get out before I sunk deeper into her.

She moaned from somewhere deep within. So deep that I felt her shuttered breaths like vibrations under my skin. She was wet. Pussy was hot. It sheathed me like a second skin. Tight fit like she had fisted my dick and started to jack me off. It didn't take us long to find our rhythm. The more dick I gave, the more she took. She wrapped her thick thighs around my waist, nails dug into my ass, and she rolled her hips in tune with my thrusts. I knew when she wanted me to go slow and be gentle by the way she would hold her breath if I went too deep. I knew when she wanted me to go harder and faster by the way she encouraged me along. I couldn't taste her as much as I wanted to. She'd told me to keep my lips to myself. But her smell was enough to whet my craving to taste her anyway. That cocoa butter scent mixed with her natural earthy musk had me dipping my head to kiss her neck anyway.

She breathlessly responded, "I said...don't put your lips on me."

I ignored her, only because each time my lips and tongue touched her neck, her walls contracted. I moved my mouth down to her perky nipples, sucked each one into my mouth. Hardened the right one, then the left. Paid them both equal attention. I made sure my tongue wrapped around each one and ravished them in kisses. She kept saying one thing, but I could feel the slippery way her body said another. I could feel my sacs tighten, dick got harder and ached with the need to release. So, I slid my hands underneath her ass cheeks, spread them wider, and I stroked deeper. Got a better feel of that spot that made her go limp and seizure all at the same time. Her lips slightly parted showing clenched teeth just before she released a soft scream of pleasure letting me know she had reached her apex. It wasn't until then that I released my own satisfaction. But I didn't stop stroking until I was sure she was sure she was satisfied.

"You do this to the Judge, too?" she asked after I rolled over.

"I don't discuss my clients with other clients."

"She's my friend."

"That's your problem."

"You enjoy fucking random women for money?"

My eyes were closed as I chuckled. "I enjoy consulting potential clients and if they seek to have me on retainer then I am more than happy to render my services."

Her breathing was so heavy it sounded as if she was panting. "Still think I'm wearing a wire?" she asked then laughed low.

"What reason would I have to suspect such a thing?

We're merely two consenting adults having fun."

"You're good."

"I'm the best."

"You have a twin, I heard."

Bitch, don't kill my vibe was what ran through my head. Silence from me was what she got.

"Does he work with you?"

"He's an attorney."

"I hear you both look just alike, but the Judge says it's something about him that makes her drawn to him like moths to a flame," she continued.

I could tell by the tone in her voice that she was fucking with me, trying to see how far she could go.

She went on to ask, "Can I meet your brother?"

"No."

"Why not?"

"He doesn't handle the same cases I do."

"Oh…I see. What if I needed an attorney?"

For a few moments all that could be heard was her heavy breathing. My chest was expanding and collapsing just the same. I didn't like to talk about my brother with my clients. It never failed that any woman I was with always wanted to know more about the elusive twin. Dionne hadn't even met him, but I guess the Judge had said enough to pique her interest. I was feeling that tinge of jealously again, but I brushed it to the side. I could hear my phone ringing then vibrating. I knew I needed to get up and answer it but also needed to relax my nerves. I sat up on the bed and looked over at Dionne. Had a good mind to flush the condom that I snatched off and leave.

She was stretched out, hands massaging her breasts as little moans escaped her mouth. I leaned down to replace her hands with my tongue. While I sucked and nibbled on her nipples, I slid my hand down between her sweaty thighs. Damn, she was still wet. I moved back over on top of her, slid down the bed until my knees were on the floor. He legs were already widened like she knew what I was about to do.

There was nothing like the smell of clean pussy. Clean pussy was healthy pussy, and my diet consisted of healthy eating. My tongue snaked out and swirled around her clit as she held herself open for me. Two of my fingers, slipped inside of her just as I sucked her clit into my mouth, hummed, and made her walls vibrate. Her hips bucked, and once again, she damn near yanked my hair out by the root. That made me stand up, still with my face buried in her pussy. I had only her shoulders on the bed as dined in.

"Ahhhh, fuck, Saigon," she yelled.

I chuckled against her clit. She'd said she refused to call me by that name,

She hissed then squealed as tremors racked her

47

body. "I…ahhh…told you not to put your lips on me…"

I pulled back and licked my lips while looking down at her. "Yeah? Tell me to stop," I dared her.

I didn't give her time to answer. She wanted me to do what she paid me to do so I would. I was so caught up in Dionne that for the first time in my history of doing what I did, I neglected another client. I stood Delana up. Had forgotten all about her while the woman who was interested in my twin— a man she had never met— grinded against my face.

It was two hours later when I left the hotel. Dionne left before I did. While I was in the bathroom, she crept out. Left more money on the table just to show me again that I was only a whore to her. I laughed and left the money there along with a note that it was a tip for someone in housekeeping to find. She'd paid me generously. I didn't need the tip. I quickly pulled out my phone and tried to call Delana back. I got no answer. I needed for her to pick up so I could give her some bullshit reason as to why I missed our meeting. I called the whole drive home and was surprised I got no answer.

"No bueno," I mumbled to myself as I pulled into my neighborhood.

My brother's shiny black Jag was in the driveway. He was still sitting in the car when I parked behind him and stepped out of mine.

"Where you been?" he asked.

His window was down. That bruise he'd gotten from Calloway was very visible underneath his eye.

"Work with a client," I answered.

He knew what that meant so he nodded as he stepped out of the car. He was dressed in a grey dress shirt and dress slacks. The only reason they were designer was because I'd taken him shopping with me, otherwise, they'd be from Wal-Mart or some shit. I looked at my mirror and saw little difference. He wore glasses. I'd finally gotten him to come around to getting some more stylish ones other than the ones that looked like our grandfather should be wearing them.

"You cut your hair," I said to him.

"Tired of getting my butt kicked for you."

"You could have fought back."

"Why? Wasn't my fight."

"Mom will be pissed."

"Mom isn't getting her butt kicked for you."

He grunted then hit the alarm on his car. My brother worked out just as much as I did, but for some reason, his clothes didn't fit him the way mine fit me. They seemed to just hang on him. Now people would be able to tell us apart. For some reason that bothered me. I thought back to Dionne and the Judge jonesing for a hit of my twin.

"What do you want?"

49

I'd asked that with a little more attitude in my voice than intended. He caught on to it. I could tell by the way he cut his eyes at me, but he didn't say anything else about it.

"Your work with your clients found me again today. For some reason Delana assumed I was you and smacked the crap out of me as I was leaving the gym. I told you not to bring your work home with you."

By home he meant that he was tired of taking the heat for me.

"That why you cut your hair?"

"Part of it."

When he reached into the car and handed me a stuffed envelope, I rolled my shoulders.

"Thank me later," he said as he walked into my house like he owned it.

Inside was the cash that Delana had intended to be for me.

"You fucked Delana?" I asked, walking into my home, and kicking the door shut behind me.

He walked into my kitchen and turned the light on. He stood in front of an 8x12 inch photo that was placed on the wall just ahead of my walk-in pantry then turned to look at me.

"You fucked Melissa. We're even."

"Did she think you were me?"

He cut his eyes at me. "For a minute."

"You told her otherwise?"

"After I was done."

I thumbed my nose and looked at the woman and child in the photo but didn't say anything. We'd never be even no matter what he said. The woman and the child in the photo proved that. Still, my brother and I sat at my kitchen table and shared dinner in silence. Delana would no longer be my client.

Four

Chapter 4

⚜

"But, Saigon, I didn't know it wasn't you until after we got done," Delana said.

"So. Doesn't matter. You slept with my brother. I can't have you on as my client anymore."

"That's not a part of the damned contract. I've read it over and over again and nowhere does it state that if I mistakenly fuck your twin brother that the contract is null and void. Don't play me."

I looked down at the paperwork lying on my desk as I listened to woman on the other end of my phone. She was right. That wasn't in the contract, but I was feeling salty.

"You knew it wasn't me, Delana. We may look alike but we are nothing alike," I said coolly.

She tsked then sighed. "I mean, yeah, the sex felt a

little different. I mean… yeah… but I just thought you were really excited to see me."

My jaw ticked. "I have to go," was all I said as I pushed end on the phone.

I didn't have time to listen to the reasons she was giving even though I knew she was right. There would always be an issue between my brother and me when it came to women. For as long as I could remember it always seemed like I went after the women who only wanted him, or he was able to capture the attention of the women I wanted through no fault of his own. My brother had always been the type to not show interest in any woman who wanted him. I guess it could be safe to say that he wanted to choose and not be chosen.

"You done?" Chad asked as he stopped at my office door.

He was dressed identical to me. It wasn't unusual that would happen with us. It was a twin thing. Most times I would dress in hopes that we didn't end up wearing the same thing, but sometimes we ended up *twinning* anyway.

I answered, "Yeah, why?"

He straightened up his form and walked into my office, dropping a file folder on my desk. "We need to go see our client. He's been charged with murder, attempted murder, and arson." Chad's voice was low and even. There was no emotion there.

53

I asked, "What's wrong with you?"

Eyes shooting daggers at me and shoulders stiff, he looked at me as if I'd offended him. "Today's Melissa's birthday."

I didn't say anything. In fact, I ignored him. For the past five years we'd been having that conversation.

"You know this man is guilty, right? Especially of murdering his wife."

"What's your point? Have we not defended the guilty before? It's what we do. It's our jobs. You've never had a problem with it before. Why now?" He was agitated. I could tell by the way he took his glasses off and cleaned off the residue that wasn't there.

"I just don't feel right about this dude."

"Well, let's talk with him first. We don't have to take the case if we don't like what we hear. So let's go." He turned and stalked away.

I sat there for a few moments to calm my nerves. The tension between us was nothing new. I looked at the picture of my wife and daughter on my desk. It had been five years since she and my daughter had walked out of our home and never came back.

Two hours later, I was on the 19th floor at the Four Seasons Hotel. Delana was sitting on my lap working her thick hips in an exotic kind of grind trying to reach the satisfaction she so desperately needed. Yeah I'd said she would no longer be my client, but she had been right to call me on that non-clause in our contractual agreement. However, she would no longer be one of my privileged clients. She would be back to where she had started. Just another client. She wouldn't get the special treatment she had once gotten. Wouldn't get the gifts or my extra time. It would just be the sex and nothing more.

My hands caressed her waist as the pump of my hips moved in tandem with her bounces. I couldn't lie and say the sex wasn't good because it was. She could ride a dick like she had been born to do it. Could suck one just the same.

"Fuck this shit is so good," she crooned out as she threw her head back.

She was into it, singing my praises like I was a god to be worshipped. The slap of her pillow soft ass against my thighs fueled the aggressiveness in my thrusts. My hands moved around to squeezed and spread her cheeks forcing her to slow down as my dick went deeper. Sweat beaded on my forehead as we christened the golden colored sofa. The blackout panels were open giving us a panoramic view of Midtown Atlanta. All anyone had to do in the office building a few yards over was grab some binoculars and they could have a free porn show.

Her breasts bounced up and down, body quivered as she yelled she was coming. "Oh my God, you two have…got to have magic dicks…"

I knew she was talking about me and my brother. She had fucked him and enjoyed it. Couldn't tell the difference between the two or so she said. I wouldn't say it angered me. It annoyed me. Maybe that was the reason I fucked her hard. Maybe that was the reason I had a hand full of her hair, gripped at the root making her take every inch I had to offer. Maybe that was the reason her soft erotic moans had turned into shrill decadent screams. She tried to control how much she could take by placing her hands on my thighs and lifting her hips, but I put a stop to that as I wrapped an arm around her waist and a hand firmly gripped the back of her neck. My tongue snaked out to capture one of her blackberry-like nipples into my mouth.

"Oh…oh shit. Slow down… oh damn, fuck, Chad"— her eyes shot open— "oh shit!"

Too late she realized her mistake and before I could stop myself, I stood and tossed her on the sofa. She fell wildly, her neck snapping back to hit the arm of the couch as her hair curtained her face. She tried to get up, but I pushed her back down, turned her over to make her knees indent the couch and her head hang forward over the back. Before she could ask what I was doing, my dick was back inside of her. Delana could never handle my dick from the behind. It didn't surprise me when she squealed, and her nails almost tore into the back covering of the couch.

"What's my name?" I asked in a tone that told I demanded an answer.

When she didn't answer fast enough, I gave her one long hard stroke, smacked her light ass so hard my handprint instantly reddened and swelled.

"Arghhh," she screamed. "Fuck!"

"What's my name?" I asked again.

Her pussy gripped me as I stopped moving. The muscles in my dick thumped causing her to moan as she tossed her hair back. "Saigon," she said breathlessly.

I pushed her head further down so she couldn't look at me. My teeth gritted as I gave her another hard stroke. "Say it again."

She did on whimpered moans and bated breaths.

Sweat dripped down my back as the muscles in my calves and thighs tightened. "Say it like you mean it."

She screamed it again all the while calling on God, his son and a few disciples. There was nothing gentle about the way I was handling her pussy, but the come that oozed and coated my dick encouraged me to keep on my journey of making sure she never got that shit twisted again. Once I was finished with her, I left her in the bed of the hotel room snoring. She never even knew when I left.

For the first time since I had been doing what I had grown to love I was feeling like my shit was falling off balance. First Saniaa messed up. Now Delana was on my shit list and I had Dionne who was to be a headache I was sure. Strangely enough the Judge hadn't called or requested my services. Why did it feel like I was losing my style?

It could have just been the day. Or it could have been that it was around the anniversary of when my wife and daughter left. I never wanted to talk about that shit. That was why I didn't go back to my office with my brother. After we left the Atlanta jail speaking with our client neither one of us said anything to one another.

Melissa used to be his girl. Then she was my girl, later becoming my wife. We had a beautiful baby girl we named Atzi because she was born in the rain. Chad never forgave me for that, even though he claimed he had. The day had been just like every year around this time between me and him. Quiet as kept; I think he grieved more than I did over her. But he was my brother, my mirror, and we had never allowed a woman to come between us on the surface. We never said anything about the underlying tension.

Later that night, I was on the Judge's arm at a society function. I guess thinking about how she hadn't called me put the vibes into the universe. It was nothing for us to show up as companions to those kinds of events because we ran in the same social circles. People were none the wiser about what went on behind closed doors.

"It always amazes me how you and that brother of yours close these cases," Judge Wagner said to me. The balding and pale man had had one too many drinks and was beginning to slur.

"We just go in and do our jobs," I told him.

The Judge stood beside me in a very flattering peach gown that contoured to her petite frame very well. The three-inch open-toed stiletto heels she had on accentuated her toned curves in all the right places.

"Yeah, but don't you have a problem with getting off slime balls?" the man asked in all seriousness.

Most of our clients were Black, those who couldn't really afford attorneys of our caliber. It was rare that we had a high-profile client like the one who called upon us today. Not to say we didn't have them on retainer. We just had more of those who couldn't afford us. So I had to wonder if they had been the corporate white collar criminals that lined his pockets would they still be slime balls.

The Judge must have seen the look on my face. "Now, now, Judge Wagner, don't go giving the young man a hard time. We need men like him and his brother in the community," she said.

Judge Wagner looked at her with his nose turned up. "But he puts these criminals, dogged animals, back on the street. You know, I think jail is the best place for those young men. They get meals and free education, a place to lay their heads at night. That's better than most of them get on the street, don't you say, Rhonda?"

The fact that he'd called her by her first name made her bat her long lashes slowly. The Judge had a real sore spot when that happened. She absolutely hated when President Obama was called simply, Barack or Mr. Obama. She felt that it was a knock at his position and title, another way for "the man" to tell him to stay in his place. She'd often felt the same when her colleagues did it to her.

None of that rocked my nerves like what Judge Wagner had said about the young men and women we kept out of the system. The Judge must have known I was about to embarrass us both in that room full of influential people because she gently tugged on my arm and led me away.

"Is that man out of his damned mind?" I asked when we were clear on the other side of the room.

Light jazz floated through the air just atop the soft murmur of the room full of people.

"Herbert is drunk," she said, blandly.

I could tell she was pissed about his affront to her as well.

"Drunk or not, his ass needs to be removed from the bench. Do you know how many cases I've tried in his courtroom? Imagine those Black and Brown young men and women that don't have me or Chad for attorneys." Although my voice was calm, I was heated.

"Can we not talk about this right now?" she asked in somberness.

The despondent look in her eyes alerted me to the fact that something else was wrong. Since she'd paid for my services, even though we were at a charity function, I put my Lothario hat on and became attentive to her. "Sure, Baby. Tell me what's wrong."

I crooked my pointing finger and lifted her chin to look up at me. I wasn't worried about her husband walking in or anyone paying too much attention to us. It wouldn't be the first time she and I had attended these kinds of events when her husband conveniently couldn't make it. It was for those very reasons she employed my services.

"He's out of town again," she said.

Water rimmed her eyes. Even though she was paying me, it pained me to see any woman in agony.

"A new girl this time?"

"Yeah. It's always a new one who makes him come home smelling himself," she said then gently moved my hand so she could cast her vision in another direction.

"He does this all the time. What's so different now?"

It took her a minute to answer. She looked toward the exit like she wanted to run away. It was rare that I saw her vulnerable side.

She huffed. "Now, he's talking about divorcing me to marry a girl younger than our youngest daughter."

She drew in a deep breath as she turned back to look at me. I could have gone into a long diatribe about how she didn't need him and how she could start life again without him. I could have told her that she was at the cusp of her career and that she needed to get rid of the dead weight before she was nominated for the Supreme Court. No one knew that little secret but me and a few others. Her husband was a Senator and knew damn well the scandal that could befall him if it leaked that he was cheating on his wife. I could have told her all of those things, but I only took her hand and lead her away from the grand ballroom of the Omni Hotel.

I'd already had the Presidential Suite booked in the North Tower of the hotel. It was her favorite room since she was able to enjoy the panoramic views of Centennial Olympic Park. When we stepped off the elevator and into the suite, I wasted to no time showing her just how special she was. To be honest, my day had been hell, too, so it would have done me some good to do her some good. That was why I peeled her gown off like layers of rose petals. She had on no bra so her perky brown breasts and raisin like nipples sat at attention for me. The lace thong she had on made the perfect V cut against her flat stomach.

"Keep the heels on," I said then nodded toward the king-sized suite.

She smiled a bright smile, but I still saw the pain in her eyes. It was my duty to take that away...if only for one night.

Later that night as I lay with the Judge sleeping peacefully in my arms, my cell buzzed. I didn't think anything of it. Just reached over and answered it.

"Speak," I answered.

"Are you available?"

"Excuse me?"

"Are you available?"

It took me a minute to recognize the smooth sexy voice on the other end of the phone, but when I did, I let out a sigh and laid back on the pillow while rubbing my eyes.

"No," I finally answered.

"Why not? Isn't it your duty to please me when I want?"

"I can see my clients by appointments only and it must be set at least two weeks in advance," I murmured.

The Judge stirred, mumbled something in her

sleep about Maurice and then fell into a silent rest again. I moved the smooth high thread count Egyptian cotton sheets back and threw my legs over the side to the floor.

"You can't make an exception to the rule? I'm willing to pay more and I really need your company right now. My pussy's wet...throbbing because I remember what you felt like between these thighs, Sai. Don't act like you don't want to fuck me," she said sassily.

I groaned low. "Dionne, you know"—I stopped and sighed— "I'm with a client right now."

She smacked her teeth and sighed harder. "Hold on."

As I waited for her to come back to the phone, I got up and walked to the bathroom. The bright lights against the white walls and cream marble floor almost blinded me. The garden tub was still wet from me and the Judge's time there. Faint traces of her juices were still on my face and lips. I turned the water on and washed my face. I placed the phone on speaker then laid it on the granite counter and kept wondering what was taking Dionne so long to come back to the phone. Then my phone buzzed alerting me to a text message. The screen lit up with Dionne's picture. I was curious as to why she was sending me a text if we were on the phone together.

I dried my hands then slid the screen to unlock it.

"Damn."

That was all I could say as the image of Dionne's fat pussy, all wet and plump with her fingers expertly showing me the juices invaded my screen.

Her sexy chuckle let me know she was back on the phone and had heard my reaction. "So why don't you come see all of that in person. I want to fuck, Sai, and only you can fuck me the way I want. I know you're with a client, but I can make it worth your while. You're with the Judge, right?"

That piqued my interest. "Why do you say that?"

My hand was already holding my throbbing dick. She had been right. That pussy sat pretty, silky wet, and golden.

"I saw you. I'm in the North Tower too, Governor's Suite. Why don't you come see about me?"

She didn't give me time to answer. She'd hung up before I could say yes or no. I had no idea she would be at the function the Judge and I were attending. As much as I knew what I was about to do was against any and all rules, my head was talking to me and I didn't mean the one on my shoulders. After I had put my clothes on, I kissed the sleeping Judge's lips and made my way to the Governor's suite.

Five

Chapter 5

I didn't have to knock. Dionne must have timed my arrival exactly because she was opening the door just as I walked up. I hadn't even taken the time to make it look like I hadn't just left another woman's bed. My slacks were only zipped and not fastened, dress shirt was partially buttoned and nowhere near the neatly tucked perfection it had been earlier. My hair flew wildly about my shoulders. The only thing that had been cleaned was the Judge's juices from my face.

I told Dionne all of that...and to my surprise, the first thing she did was drop down to her knees, snatch my pants down and take my dick into her mouth. I'd told her I needed to shower. It was as if it had fallen on deaf ears. I had just gone knee deep inside of the Judge for three rounds. Dionne only looked up at me and smirked as she made eye contact while swirling her tongue around the head of my manhood. The way she was squatting gave me plenty view of her breasts and the fact that she was playing with herself at the same time.

Two things that had my mind in a daze: one was that I couldn't understand how Dionne had remained faithful to her husband all those years with the hunger of her sexual appetite, and two, I'd never had my dick swallowed the way she was swallowing it. I wasn't one to brag on the size and length of my manhood, but I knew I was a heavyweight in the game. Dionne took my dick in both hands, swallowed it all the way back and still found room for my balls. And she was nasty like a porn star with it. Her mouth was wet and hot just like her pussy had been the first time I had it. It had me wanting to test how she would feel without the condom...but that was a no go.

I needed something to hold on to as I could feel my toes throwing gang signs in my shoes. The muscles in my ass and the back of my thighs burned because at times her mouth game was so good, she had me standing on my toes. By the time she pushed me down on the sofa behind me, I was releasing my first round. She moved her face and stroked me. I watched through blurry vision as my cream flowed through her fingers.

"It looks healthy. I would taste it but…you're not my husband," she said. As she stood, she held her come covered hand out then smiled.

"You just sucked my dick. Shouldn't that have been left to your husband, too?" I asked sarcasm dripping.

Dionne was still the type who liked to play with a man's head. Yeah, she wanted a good dick down, but she still wanted to toy with my pride so she could feel better about what she was doing. She rolled her eyes then disappeared around the corner into the bathroom. I could only assume she was washing her hands while I sat there holding dick in my hands. I was still hard, still had life that I needed her to zap from me.

I stood and removed my shoes then all of my clothes. I hit the corner to the bathroom and found her standing at the sink, with her cell phone on the counter. She was calling someone. She had the phone on speaker so obviously she didn't give a damn about me being in the room. When a man answered, and her eyes widened seeing me standing the doorway naked, stroking my dick, I knew it was her husband.

"I just wanted to call and let you know I'd be home tomorrow. I'm a bit drunk and don't feel like the drive back home tonight."

The man's voice sounded gruff, like he had just

been awakened from his sleep. "You need me to come and get you?"

Her eyes stayed on mine as I sauntered up behind her. I slid her long ponytail to the side then placed a kiss on that place between her shoulder and neck. She bit down on her bottom lip but didn't tell me to stop. I grabbed the golden wrapped condom she had hidden in her palm, ripped it open and expertly slid it on.

"No..no...I'm fine. Rhonda and I are sharing a hotel room here at the hotel," she lied.

I placed my hand on the back of her neck and urging her to bend over the sink like I wanted. Her ass arched up perfectly. That arch put a dip in her back that had me licking my lips wanting to place kisses on the heart shaped rump. I placed one of her thick thighs on the countertop then slid hard into her with no remorse. Her legs shook and a fist pounded the counter. She should have been mindful that her husband was still on the phone. My thighs smacked against her ass as she sneered at me under eyed through the mirror. I didn't give a shit. She called me to fuck her so that was what I would do.

"Baby, you okay? What was that?" her husband asked.

She hissed, tried to stifle a moaned as her walls breathed around me. "I hit my toe. Got...ah... didn't turn the light on as I was using the restroom." I smirked at the way her hands gripped the edges of the counter, then at the way one had grabbed at the door panel.

"Well, go rest. I'll call to check on you later. I love you, Dionne."

"Ohhh fuck," she whispered as I fisted her ponytail and snatched her head up.

With my knees bent and a hump in my back, I stroked with a madness that said her pussy was good even with the barrier between us.

"Baby?" he called.

"Sorry, Derek, baby. Was taking my…"—she gave the sexiest low growl— "was taking my dress off," she continued to lie. "I love you too, Honey."

When she finally hung up the phone, I flipped her around, sat her plentiful ass on the counter and made her look at me as I slowed my stroke.

"You know, you ain't shit," I mocked her.

She smacked my face, hard. The sting of the opened palm assault pissed me off. I didn't like to be hit in my face. It caught me off guard, so much so that my hand found its way around her neck. Through gritted teeth and hard deep penetrating strokes, I fucked her as I choked her semi-conscious.

She was panting…somewhere between an orgasm and being lightheaded as she tapped aggressively on my hand.

"Safe…safe word…" was all she could get out, but

I knew what she meant.

Although we hadn't established that we were into that kinky BDSM shit, I knew she was telling me she'd had enough. I let her go. My dick slid out of her and swung like a pendulum. I hadn't busted my second nut, but as long as she'd gotten hers, my job was done. I got a look at myself in passing as I glanced in the mirror. A sheen of sweat coated my golden tinted body. Dionne sat looking at me like she was seeing me for the first time. I grunted as I walked out of the bathroom and headed back to the sofa. I plopped my naked ass down, dick still sheathed in the Trojan Magnum that was beginning to feel too small.

I gave an outright grin when Dionne stumbled from the bathroom. She leaned against the archway. "Why did you do that?" she asked.

"Do what?"

"That? I was on the phone with my husband."

"So."

"You're a dick."

"You're a pussy."

"That wasn't funny."

"I wasn't laughing, and neither were you."

I patted my thighs and signaled for her to come cop a squat on me. She was talking a good game, but I had turned the tables on her. I could tell by the way her breathing was shallow that she wanted more. That hunger was still in her eyes, the need to be dominated sexually. She had walked over and was just about to straddle my lap when a knock at the door stopped us. She looked from the door to me, then from me to the door.

"Who is that?" I asked, not really caring.

She shrugged. "I don't know."

"You and your husband live near here?"

She shook her head. "No. That wouldn't be him."

I watched as she slowly walked to the door. My eyes were trained on her ass the whole time. She stood on her toes and looked through the peephole.

My curiosity was piqued when she opened the door completely naked. "Yeah?" she asked the person standing on the other side.

"You infringed on my time with him. Not cool."

It was the Judge.

"I was going to send him back."

"You're paying him extra, for mine and your time because of this."

Dionne's face frowned and she rolled her neck. "Bitch, whatever. Your old-ass was asleep, and I needed some dick."

The Judge slapped the door and Dionne stumbled back. There was a look on her face that said they would have been scrapping if I had not been sitting there, hair wild, dick in my hand.

The Judge walked in and got in Dionne's face. "You

just always got to have what I have, huh…bitch?"

My brows arched because that was unusual for her to ever be so out of character. I saw she had changed into a thin spaghetti strapped shirt and yoga pants. She wore anything well with the way her body was made.

"Oh, like you stole Maurice from me in college?" Dionne shot back.

"Like you didn't go after Derek," the Judge countered then laughed. "We see who got the short end of that deal."

Dionne's upper lip twitched as she placed her hands on her naked hips. "I would say you got it the shortest since Maurice is fucking everybody but you."

It was one thing for me to be sitting there watching two women of their caliber fighting over me, but it was something else altogether when the Judge reached out and slapped Dionne so hard that I thought she had pissed herself. Now some may have asked why I didn't get up to stop them. One, that didn't have shit to do with me. Money from both of them had already been delivered to my account. Two, since neither one of them was sitting on my dick at the moment; the scene was good porn to stroke my dick to.

Now what I wasn't expecting was for Dionne to snatch the judge by her hair and back her up against the wall. I thought they were about to go fisticuffs until she roughly took the Judge's mouth.

"Damn," was my reaction with heightened curiosity.

The Judge's shirt came off quickly before Dionne was going for her pants. I didn't know what kind of fight and fuck freaky thing they had going on, but a brother sat up so he could get a better view of the action. I grunted when Dionne knelt, threw the Judge's chocolate thigh over her shoulder and went in like she was famished as she performed oral sex on her. I didn't know what turned me on more, two beautiful women sharing that sexual intimacy with one another or when the Judge crooked her finger and invited me to the show.

I didn't know what to think of what was going on in front of me. I felt as if they had planned that shit. The way they took turns doing things to my body, from the sucking to the licking, had me wondering just how many times they had done this. I'd gone and broken another one of my rules. There was never to be another woman in the room when I was with one client, but the Judge and Dionne had me feeling like a king. From the way the Judge knelt and took me skillfully into her mouth to the way Dionne had positioned herself on my shoulders at the same time so I could eat her out, the night was one none of us would forget.

Six

Chapter 6

༄༅

The next few days found me working from home. Couldn't deal with my brother's mood swings. We'd decided to take on the client from before. I was dead set against it because that man had guilt written all over him. I mean, yeah, we had dealt with clients who had murder charges before, but this guy didn't have one ounce of remorse for what he had done. Then to think he had traveled across state lines to do more dirt?

I guess it annoyed me more so because normally my brother and I would agree on when and when not to take on clients. This time, it was like because I'd said no, he'd said yes. That had never happened, and it worried me.

"Are you going to the luncheon today?" Chad

asked after he had, once again, walked into my crib like he owned it.

I wasn't tripping on that part because I normally did the same to him. I was tripping because he had a scowl on his face that said he was still on his bullshit.

"No," I answered from behind my home office desk. "We have to prepare to fly to Florida in a few days or did you forget?"

"Shouldn't you be asking yourself that question? Don't you have a meeting of the male Lotharios and gigolos? Had no idea you were actually going for the legitimate business."

He'd been saying little snide remarks like that for the last few days. Normally my brother was quiet and reserved, and normally he would have grieved Melissa and Atzi with me and got over it in a day or so. This year I felt like something else was bothering him.

"Yo, why you coming at me like that, Chad? So, we got beef now?"

I asked him that in the slang that, often, some of our clients used. As I said, my brother and I were night and day. He was always prim and proper while I was anything but.

"I don't even know what 'got beef" means," he asked, using his fingers as quotations. "Just wanting to make sure your priorities were in order."

"My shit's always in order."

"I'm not so sure. If you'd been where you were supposed to be, we'd still have Melissa and Atzi here with us now, wouldn't we?"

I dropped my pen, thumbed my nose, and gave a curt chuckle. "So, we're still on this shit? We're still on you feeling some type of way about *my* wife and *my* daughter?"

I put emphasis on the *my* part both times just so he could get the point.

My brother's light grayish blue eyes darkened behind his glasses. If there had ever been one woman he loved, it was Melissa. He never got over losing her to me. When he was on his way to becoming junior partner at Hayes & Wacoby, one of the top criminal law firms in the country, he'd put in long hours at work. My brother had always been great at what he did. Even though we'd gone to two different colleges we'd still made a name for ourselves. Our initial plan hadn't been to own our own law firm. In fact, when he got with Melissa, I wasn't even sure if I wanted to use my law degree.

Still, my brother was headfirst taking cases, winning them, becoming the big man on campus so to speak, all the while neglecting Melissa. I remember the first night he called me and asked me if I could pick Melissa up and take her home because he wasn't able to leave the office like he'd planned. That was the best and worst night of my life. The best night

77

because Melissa and I started a friendship that would lead us down the road of betrayal. The worst because that was the night I almost lost my bond with my brother.

"She wasn't *your* daughter," he said in a low and even tone to me.

My head gave a slight jerk as I tilted it. "Say what?"

"Melissa was *your* wife but Atzi wasn't *your* daughter."

I took a deep swallow, sat back in my desk chair, and closed my hand around my mouth. My arms started to shake. No, fuck that. My whole body shook, heart swelled and thumped to the point I thought it would jump out my chest. Water blurred my vision.

"What the fuck you saying to me, Chad?"

There was a stoic look on his face. One that I couldn't read. I couldn't tell whether he was getting a kick out of fucking with me or if he was telling the truth.

"I'm saying Atzi was *my* daughter. Melissa told me six months before they died."

I gave a heavy, disheartened chuckle. "You were fucking my wife?"

"She was mine first."

My teeth sunk down into my bottom lip, legs started bouncing one after the other as my fists balled, and teeth started to grind. In the back of my mind, I'd always wondered if Melissa was ever really over my brother. Did I believe she loved me? Yes. But there was always this feeling that told me the love she had for him was still there. I just didn't listen to it. Pushed that shit to the back of my mind for it never to be brought up again... because I was a man in love with a woman who was secretly still in love with my brother.

"For how long?" I asked in a low growl.

"For as long as you were having sex with her behind my back."

For the first time ever in our existence I felt the urge to jump up and put my brother on his ass. Even though his face was emotionless as it always was, I still saw the storm brewing behind his eyes. I stood and kicked my chair back. Chad's gaze never faltered. Why now? Why was he telling me this now?

"You needed to know." I hadn't even realized I'd asked those questions out loud. Chad continued, "You walk around like you're above reproach, like you can just do what you want without consequences, from screwing other men's wives and girlfriends to—"

"But she was my wife. We went beyond just boyfriend and girlfriend, Brother. Are you fucking kidding me?" I yelled. "Atzi wasn't my kid?"—Tears had rimmed my eyes and started to fall— "Please tell me you're fucking with me, Chad."

"She was bringing her to see me when they died," he said solemnly. "Would have probably made it if you hadn't called her and made her turn around to go back to pick you up from the airport. Why couldn't you have just stayed in Florida like you were supposed to?"

Something in me snapped. Memories from that day started to flash before my eyes. Before I was in the business of pleasing women, I was a married man. I had been in Florida on business with a client, but just needed to get to home to see my wife and daughter. Atzi had been very sick and Chad had been working with another client back home. It had been my turn to take the consultation with an out-of-town client. Things started to make sense. I finally figured out the reason he'd called and blacked out on me over the phone about not handling my business with the client.

Those times when Melissa would look like she was in another time and place, those times when I would catch her staring at me, she had a look in her eyes that was empty. Then there were those unexplained absences, the nervousness when we thought Azti would need a bone marrow transplant because she had sickle cell anemia. It was all because she knew that there was a possibility that I wouldn't have been able to donate the marrow because she wasn't my daughter. My heart caved in when thoughts of my daughter being a diabetic stabbed at me. It wasn't just because the shit ran in the family. It was because, her father, real father, Chad was a diabetic.

Before I could stop myself, I jumped my desk like it was a hurdle and went after my brother like he was the enemy. His right jab caught my eye followed by a left hook before mine could land. My brother wasn't a fighter but that didn't mean he couldn't fight. As kids I'd been on the receiving end of his fist many times. But we weren't kids anymore. His punches backed me up, but they didn't floor me. His mistake. I ducked a swing, hit him with a rib shot that almost buckled his knees, then another punch to the left of his face. His glasses went flying one way and him another. I rushed him, but he did some kind of ninja move that made him end up behind me. When I turned, he rushed at me. His arms enclosed around my torso, lifting me from my feet and slamming me on the floor of my office.

I was fucked in a ground and pound fight with my brother and, I knew it. However, he didn't have his glasses. That meant he couldn't see and was going off of pure instinct. Chad's face was flushed red as I was sure mine was. His eyes darkened and watered as he bit down, bared his teeth, and drew back to land a punch in my face that rearranged the contact in my right eye. Pain ripped through my skull causing

81

me more fury.

When we were teenaged boys fighting under my parents' roof, it was nothing for our pops to come snatch us apart and threaten to kill us if we made another threatening step toward the other again. Pops wasn't around now though. I tried to flip Chad off me, but he had been trained in this type of combat so it didn't work.

Another one of his blows was about to land until I quickly moved my face. Because laying on my hair was pinning me down, his fist still brushed my face. I knew Chad could win the fight at this point, so I went for an old war wound he had from back when he first went to college in LA. He'd been shot in the shoulder by a racist cop. The bullet was still lodged in his shoulder and sometimes caused him great pain.

I saw my opening when he moved back to try to put me in a submission maneuver. My left fist came up and landed a blow to his shoulders that made him fall back. He jerked back and roared with pain. Although he was hurting, which was evident by the way he was holding his shoulder and by the way he had yelled, we were both back to our feet quickly.

Both of us stood on opposite sides of the room staring each other down. Neither one wanting to go another round. It was exhausting fighting that nigga. I'd never win, but I would also never give up. He knew that. My right eye lid kept fluttering and it was burning due the fact that my contact was moving around each time I blinked. I was sure Chad could only see the blurry outline of me because he couldn't see two paces in front of him without his glasses. For the first time in our brotherhood, we'd come to blows over a woman. It had me feeling like shit. I took a moment to remove my contact then place it back in correctly.

"I need my glasses," he pleaded through bated breaths.

He wiped a bloody knuckle across his nose and his gaze darted around. I looked to my right and saw them lying just underneath my desk. "I ain't giving you shit until you tell me the truth."

He stooped over holding his shoulder when he yelled, "I told you. I told you the freaking truth. Now help me find my glasses. Please!" For reasons no one ever knew, Chad panicked when he didn't have his glasses on.

I spit the blood in my mouth on the floor. "Not helping you find shit. You found your way into my wife's pussy, find your glasses."

He snarled. "Fucking prick. It was more like she found her way to me. I didn't come for her. I never went after her. She came back to me."

He'd cursed, something he rarely did, if ever. His chest was heaving up and down just like mine. His

83

words stung like hell because I knew in my heart my brother was telling the truth. To know my wife had left my bed and then sought out my brother's was a bullet I didn't want to bite. Then I imagined how he'd felt when the shoe was on the other foot. Chad had never as much as looked at me with evil in his eyes when he found out me and Melissa were in love.

We'd argued. He and Melissa had even passed a few words, but after a few weeks, he gave us his blessings and then threw himself back into work. He'd told me he'd chalked it all up to her never having loved him in the first place. For months afterwards I was always trying to make sure he was okay with it. What I had done was some treacherous shit, no doubt. My mother had threatened to go up side my head, but in the end, my brother and I were still closer than close. He'd even stood in as my best man at the wedding. That was an awkward moment for all parties involved, but Chad, my older brother by ten minutes, assured me all was well.

Through all of that nothing hurt as much as knowing Atzi wasn't my child. That knowledge had gripped my heart in its fist and was threatening to squeeze the life from me.

I asked him, "Why didn't you tell me? You knew that shit for six fucking months before they were killed, Chad, and you didn't tell me, why?"

"You knew you and Melissa were sleeping with each other for over a year and you didn't tell me, why?"

"This shit is different, Chad. Atzi…she was my daughter!"

"Melissa was my woman. I loved her. You knew how much I loved her. That didn't stop you. Did it?"— Chad stopped talking and finally stood straight up—"Karma doesn't care how she gets you back. It's like a rubber band. You can only stretch it so far before it comes back and smacks you in the face."

Although I knew most of the water in his eyes came from the fact that he needed his glasses, I still saw and heard the hurt and truth behind his words. Yeah, he was right, but to me, Atzi not being my daughter was a more serious charge than me taking his girl. For eight years I'd loved that little girl. That was my kid, my daughter, and to tell me that the last six months of her life Chad knew she was his daughter and not mine burned like scalding hot water. I knew it was childish, but I picked up his glasses and placed them on the top of the bookshelf against the wall. Then, because I know he couldn't see, I rushed him, gave him a blow to his face that dropped him to one knee. As the blood spewed from his nose, I stalked away from my office and home in a fit of rage.

* * *

It took me three days to speak to my brother again. Three days and long nights for me to answer any phone calls or take on any clients. I was an emotional wreck. I couldn't get over the fact that Atzi wasn't my daughter. I reasoned that she looked like me, looked like my spitting image, but so did my damned twin brother. For three days I replayed the years we'd been blessed with her presence on this earth and the more I thought about her, the more I saw my brother in her. That girl would read a book from sunup to sundown. She was a genius in math already at the age of five. She could look at a math equation and solve it without blinking. She was computer literate and could solve a puzzle in seconds.

While I was a smart man, I was nowhere near the Mensa my brother was. Through the tears, hurt, and mind-altering anger, I finally admitted it to myself. Atzi was his daughter and not mine. Just like Chad had to suck it up and face the facts about me and Melissa, it was my turn to do the same. That shit cut me to the core of the man I was.

As I stood at my wife's and daughter's grave sites—she would forever be remembered by me as my daughter— I finally understood the reason every year my brother grieved just as much as I did. That was why it wasn't a surprise that I looked up and he

86

was standing by my side.

"You found your glasses, I see," I said.

The wind blew around us as the gray clouds moved in overhead. It was about to pour down raining, just as it was the day a motorcycle cut my wife off on the expressway sending her into a tailspin that inevitably caused a Dodge Ram pickup to T-bone her, push her car into another lane for a big rig to finish her and my daughter off.

Chad and I stood side by side, once again dressed the same, in designer black dress slacks, blood red button downs, and wing tipped black dress shoes. The only differences were his glasses and haircut. We'd even brought their favorite flowers, carnations, to adorn their headstones.

"Yeah, had to blindly find my way to my car and grab my spare before going back into the house to see where you had put the others," he said.

After that was a long silence. One that was serenaded by passing traffic, birds flying above us, and the whistling of the wind.

"I'm sorry," Chad said.

I looked over at my older brother. No matter how many times we'd fought, and even when it was my fault, he always apologized first.

"So am I."

That was how we always squashed our fights. A few hours later we sat at the St. Regis Bar of the

St. Regis Hotel in Atlanta; both of us a little lit, but neither of us man enough to admit it first. Chad was probably embarrassed at his inebriated state because he was the good twin. Me? I wouldn't admit it because, for once, I got to see him act out of character. The bar was crowded for the middle of the week. Walk-in patrons and hotel guests alike were drinking and being merry. Chad and I had decided to come to this bar because of the need to get away from our side of town and because it was easy to get to once we left from seeing our client again.

"You get with Delana again?" he asked out the blue after we had watched the seductive sway of a sister's hip as she exited the establishment.

It took me a couple seconds to answer because honey's backside was sitting so pretty and right in that white belted body-hugging dress she had on.

But I finally answered, "Yeah."

It wasn't often my brother and I got to sit and chat like the best friends we were, but when we did, the time was enjoyed.

Chad said, "Her body and skills are immaculate."

"She gave a pretty hefty tip. You must have put some shit on her."

"Hadn't had sex in a while. She was beautiful and willing."

"She thought you were me."

"Yeah… until she got ready to orgasm."

The obtuse jazz music in the place was annoying. The dim lighting was putting me in the mood for some loving. Mix that with the rain outside, the warm bourbon—and I was anxious to fall between some soft thighs. After I'd turned my private phone back on, I had messages from all my clients wanting to know where I had disappeared to, all except for the Judge and Dionne. They had crossed my mind a lot.

After seeing the way they licked and slurped at the other's body then did the same to mine had my dick slowly rising. I moved around on the stool then slyly adjusted my dick much to the chagrin of one of the ladies sitting in the booth across from us and to the liking of her friends smirking at me. I winked at the ladies and turned my attention back to my brother.

"Is that your real hair?"

I was about to counter what he had said about Delana until a smooth chocolate sister caught my attention. She was standing in heels that made her tower over me while I sat. Her long chocolate legs had me licking my lips. Although she was talking to me, Chad's eyes were zeroed in on her round juicy derriere. Her smile was bright. There was a slight gap in her upper teeth, but nothing that would make her less beautiful. She was wearing no make-up, had slight scarring to her cheeks from acne, but still fine none the less. Her succulent lips shone with just enough gloss to make me imagine what they would feel like wrapped around my dick.

"Why wouldn't it be?" I asked her snidely, just wanting to play her game of cat and mouse.

She shrugged her rounded shoulders and moved her golden clutch from under one arm to the other. "You know, in Atlanta, you can never be too sure about what's real and what's fake."

I studied her. Glanced at Chad who took his eyes off her ass long enough to flash me a look. I smirked. "This is my hair, beautiful lady, all of it," I assured her.

"Can I touch it?"

I turned on my stool, with one legged propped on the bar of the stool and the other on the floor. "That depends."

She saw the look in my eyes and her smile got wider. "On what?"

"If you're going to let me touch something in return..."

Chad chuckled behind her causing her to turn around. Her eyes widened when she looked at him. "Oh— oh my gosh! Are you two twins?" she asked, all excited as she looked from me to him.

"Our birth certificates say so," he answered.

I swear that woman swooned when she heard my brother's voice.

"Damn, you two are fucking gorgeous. And…ah…what are you trying to touch?" she asked then glanced around before casting her gaze back on me then Chad.

I let my eyes roam her body from head to toe then back up again. Her shape was beautiful. She was country-thick and wore her weight well. "Whatever you give me permission to touch."

"You can touch me anywhere you'd like…" She said that then pushed some of her hair behind her right ear as she blushed.

Most of the men around the area openly admired her while some of the women wished they had been brave enough to be in her shoes.

"Then, yes you can touch my hair," I finally told her.

"And can I touch his too?"

She was looking from me to Chad. Each time her eyes fell on him she visibly shivered where she stood. Behind his glasses, he never took his eyes off of her. His gaze found mine and a silent message passed between the two of us. I stood, brushing my body in close proximity to hers. Her breath caught as she craned her neck to look up at me.

"Damn, you're tall," she expressed in awe.

Chad stood behind her. We'd caged her in. Something we often did to women when we got into our moods to share.

My lights eyes stared hungrily down at her. "Go on, touch it," I told her.

She couldn't figure out if I was talking about my hair or my dick since her eyes kept going to the latter.

"Yeah, touch mine, too," Chad said.

The woman was flushed. Even though her skin was dark, I saw the red underneath her cheeks. If I had looked around the room, I would have seen that all eyes were on us and the dark-skinned beauty. She was chocolate enclosed in caramel.

The woman fanned herself with her hand. "Whew," she exclaimed then reached up to stroke my hair.

When her fingers touched my scalp, for the hell of it, I growled low in my throat. She jumped back bumping right into my twin's solid frame. His hands found her waist and he moved closer to her, completely sandwiching her between us.

"Oh Lord, Jesus, it's a fire," she semi-joked, using the quote made famous by a lady on YouTube.

My right hand found my way to caress the side of her face. The pad of my thumb stroked her cheek before I dipped my head to kiss the vein pulsating in her neck on one side while Chad did the same to the other side from behind. Cat calls laced the bar. The bartender, a friend of ours, shook his head and chuckled. If we'd wanted, we could have made

Ms. Chocolate Thick Booty do whatever we had in mind, but as her chest heaved up and down, I could tell she wasn't ready. I also knew she had creamed her panties by the way her lips trembled, and her breath caught.

After the little show, we sat back down on our stools, picked up our drinks and nodded to the woman. I could tell she wasn't sure on how she was supposed to act or react. It was quite comical to the both of us to see her standing there with a dreamy look in her eyes trying to figure out if she should rent a room and ask us to join her later. Chad and I had always had the power to render a woman speechless.

Now, the ball was in her court...

Seven

Interlude

ey, I told you I would pull out just as you craved for more, didn't I? I gave you fair warning. My life is complicated. My brother and I share a bond that many wouldn't understand. We're more than brothers. We're twins.

Yo, do me a favor though, don't send me any messages through Nikki-Michelle asking about my brother, a'ight? I'm not trying to introduce him to any of you or bring him into my business. And no, I'm not jealous of him. Why would I be? I mean we look just alike.

Delana still has me shaking my damn head. How in hell did she think he was me? I mean, how could she not tell the difference? Whatever. It was what it was. If Nikki-Michelle is lucky, I'll allow her to finish telling you my story another time and place.

Until then, I have to go. There is a naked woman in my hotel bed, caramel thick thighs spread open, beautiful smile on her face. Nadine is her name. She's plus-sized; thick and warm in all the right places. I love her smile. Shit's infectious. I'm going to enjoy doing her while you enjoy reminiscing about how wet I got you. Until next time…when you get that feeling and need sexual healing…call me.

About the Author

Nikki-Michelle resides in Metro- Atlanta, Georgia by way of Lexington, Mississippi. Carried by her love of reading, she began writing at the early age of twelve and has been on a journey of "trying" to pen the perfect novel ever since (she's still working on that). Her love of writing and wanting to create fiction with true to life situations are what inspire her to continue to write stories readers will enjoy with characters they can relate to.

You can catch her works in the previously released anthologies 'If Only For One Night 1&2,' 'Full Figured 3', and 'Girls From Da Hood 7'. Her full-length works include 'Tell Me No Secrets' and 'Tell Me No Lies' 'All the Things I'm Missing at Home' and the critically acclaimed, Bi-Satisfied &

Bi-Sensual.

She's also dabbled in the Fantasy genre as she co-authored 'Promised Land' with Essence best-selling author, Brenda Hampton.

You can connect with me on:

🌐 https://www.nikkimichellebooks.com

📘 https://www.facebook.com/nikkimichellereaders

Made in United States
Orlando, FL
08 December 2022

25863565R00059